For my brother, Pieter.
Our story, in a way.
M.M.

For my parents
F.S.

This is a work of fiction. Names, characters, places and incidents
are either the product of the author's imagination or, if real, are
used fictitiously. First published 2000 in *From Hereabout Hill*.
This edition published 2015 by Walker Books Ltd, 87 Vauxhall
Walk, London SE11 5HJ • 10 9 8 7 6 5 4 3 2
Text © 2000 Michael Morpurgo • Illustrations © 2015 Felicita Sala
The right of Michael Morpurgo and Felicita Sala to be identified
as author and illustrator respectively of this work has been asserted
by them in accordance with the Copyright, Designs and Patents
Act 1988 • This book has been typeset in Bembo • Printed in China
All rights reserved. No part of this book may be reproduced,
transmitted or stored in an information retrieval system in any
form or by any means, graphic, electronic or mechanical, including
photocopying, taping and recording, without prior written
permission from the publisher • British Library Cataloguing in
Publication Data: a catalogue record for this book is available from
the British Library • ISBN 978-1-4063-0657-6 • www.walker.co.uk

Tracking down a polar bear shouldn't be that difficult. You just follow the paw prints. My father is a polar bear. Now if *you* had a father who was a polar bear, you'd be curious, wouldn't you? You'd go looking for him. That's what I did, I went looking for him, and I'm telling you he wasn't at all easy to find.

In a way I was lucky, because I always had two fathers. I had a father who *was* there – I called him Douglas – and one who wasn't there, the one I'd never even met – the polar bear one. Yet in a way he was there. All the time I was growing up he was there inside my head. But he wasn't only in my head, he was at the bottom of a Start-Rite shoebox, our secret treasure box with the rubber bands round it, which I kept hidden at the bottom of the cupboard in our bedroom. So how, you might ask, does a polar bear fit into a shoebox? I'll tell you.

My big brother Terry first showed me the magazine under the bedclothes, by torchlight, in 1948 when I was five years old. The magazine was called *Theatre World*. I couldn't read it at the time, but he could.

(He was two years older than me, and already mad about acting and the theatre and all that – he still is.) He had saved up all his pocket money to buy it. I thought he was crazy. "A shilling! You can get about a hundred lemon sherbets for that down at the shop," I told him.

Terry just ignored me and turned to page twenty-seven. He read it out: "'*The Snow Queen*, a dramat – something or other – of Hans Andersen's famous story, by the Young Vic Company.'" And there was a large black and white photograph right across the page – a photograph of two fierce-looking polar bears baring their teeth and about to eat two children, a boy and a girl, who looked very frightened.

"Look at the polar bears," said Terry. "You see

that one on the left, the fatter one? That's our dad,
our real dad. It says his name and everything – Peter
Van Diemen. But you're not to tell. Not Douglas,
not even Mum, promise?"

"My dad's a polar bear?" I said. I was a little confused.

"Promise you won't tell," he went on, "or I'll give you a Chinese burn."

Of course I wasn't going to tell, Chinese burn or no Chinese burn. I was hardly going to go to school the next day and tell everyone that I had a polar bear for a father, was I? And I certainly couldn't tell my mother, because I knew she never liked it if I ever asked about my real father. She always insisted that Douglas was the only father I had. I knew he wasn't, not really. So did she, so did Terry, so did Douglas. But for some reason that was always a complete mystery to me, everyone in the house pretended that he was.

Some background might be useful here. I was born, I later found out, when my father was a soldier in

Baghdad during the Second World War. (You didn't know there were polar bears in Baghdad, did you?) Sometime after that my mother met and fell in love with a dashing young officer in the Royal Marines called Douglas MacLeish.

All this time, evacuated to the Lake District away from the bombs, blissfully unaware of the war and Douglas, I was learning to walk and talk and do my business in the right place at the right time. So my father came home from the war to discover that his place in my mother's heart had been taken. He did all he could to win her back. He took her away on a week's cycling holiday in Suffolk to see if he could rekindle the light of their love.

But it was hopeless. By the end of the week they had come to an amicable arrangement. My father would simply disappear, because he didn't want to "get in the way". They would get divorced quickly and quietly, so that Terry and I could be brought up as a new family with Douglas as our father. Douglas would adopt us

and give us MacLeish as our surname. All my father insisted upon was that Terry and I should keep Van Diemen as our middle name. That's what happened. They divorced. My father disappeared, and at the age of three I became Andrew Van Diemen MacLeish. It was a mouthful then and it's a mouthful now.

So Terry and I had no actual memories of our father whatsoever. I do have some vague recollections of standing on a railway bridge somewhere near Earls Court in London, where we lived, with Douglas's sister – Aunty Betty, as I came to know her – telling us that we had a brand new father who'd be looking after us from now on.

I was really not that concerned, not at the time. I was much more interested in the train that was chuffing along under the bridge, wreathing us in a fog of smoke.

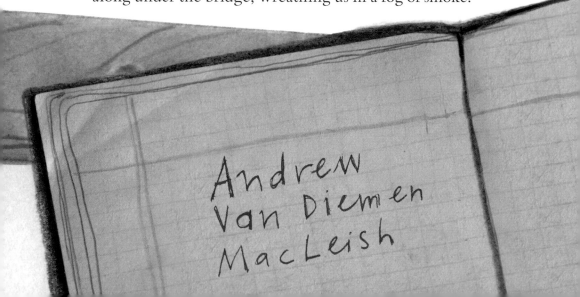

Andrew
Van Diemen
MacLeish

My first father, my real father, my missing father,
became a taboo person, a big hush–hush taboo person
that no one ever mentioned, except for Terry and me.
For us he soon became a sort of secret phantom father.

We used to whisper about him under the blankets at night. Terry would sometimes go snooping in my mother's desk and he'd find things out about him. "He's an actor," Terry told me one night. "Our dad's an actor, just like Mum is, just like I'm going to be."

It was only a couple of weeks later that he brought the theatre magazine home. After that we'd take it out again and look at our polar bear father. It took some time, I remember, before the truth of it dawned on me – I don't think Terry can have explained it very well. If he had, I'd have understood it much sooner, I'm sure I would. The truth, of course – as I think you might have guessed by now – was that my father was both an actor *and* a polar bear at one and the same time.

Douglas went out to work a lot and when he was home he was a bit silent, so we didn't really get to know him. But we did get to know Aunty Betty. Aunty Betty simply adored us, and she loved giving us treats. She wanted to take us on a special Christmas treat, she said. Would we like to go to the zoo? Would we like to go

to the pantomime? There was *Dick Whittington* or *Puss in Boots*. We could choose whatever we liked.

Quick as a flash, Terry said, "*The Snow Queen*. We want to go to *The Snow Queen*."

So there we were a few days later, Christmas Eve 1948, sitting in the stalls at a matinée performance of *The Snow Queen* at the Young Vic theatre, waiting, waiting for the moment when the polar bears come on. We didn't have to wait for long. Terry nudged me and pointed, but I knew already which polar bear my father had to be. He was the best one, the snarliest one, the growliest one, the scariest one. Whenever he came on he really looked as if he was going to eat someone, anyone. He looked mean and hungry and savage, just the way a polar bear should look.

I have no idea whatsoever what happened in *The Snow Queen*. I just could not take my eyes off my polar bear father's curling claws, his slavering tongue, his killer eyes. My father was without doubt the finest

polar bear actor the world had ever seen. When the great red curtains closed at the end and opened again for the actors to take their bows, I clapped so hard that my hands hurt. Three more curtain calls and the curtains stayed closed. The safety curtain came down and my father was cut off from me, gone, gone for ever. I'd never see him again.

Terry had other ideas. Everyone was getting up, but Terry stayed sitting. He was staring at the safety curtain as if in some kind of trance. "I want to meet the polar bears," he said quietly.

Aunty Betty laughed. "They're not bears, dear, they're actors, just actors, people acting. And you can't meet them, it's not allowed."

"I want to meet the polar bears," Terry repeated.

So did I, of course, so I joined in. "Please, Aunty Betty," I pleaded. "Please."

"Don't be silly. You two, you do get some silly notions sometimes. Have a choc ice instead. Get your coats on now."

So we each got a choc ice. But that wasn't the end of it.

We were in the foyer caught in the crush of the crowd when Aunty Betty suddenly noticed that Terry was missing. She went loopy. Aunty Betty always wore a fox stole, heads still attached, round her shoulders. Those poor old foxes looked every bit as pop-eyed and frantic as she did, as she plunged through the crowd, dragging me along behind her and calling for Terry.

Gradually the theatre emptied. Still no Terry. There was quite a to-do, I can tell you. Policemen were called in off the street. All the programme sellers joined in the search, everyone did. Of course, I'd worked it out. I knew exactly where Terry had gone, and what he was up to.

By now Aunty Betty was sitting down in the foyer
and sobbing her heart out. Then, cool as a cucumber,
Terry appeared from nowhere, just wandered into the
foyer. Aunty Betty crushed him to her in a great hug.
Then she went loopy all over again, telling him what
a naughty, naughty boy he was, going off like that.
"Where were you? Where have you been?" she cried.

"Yes, young man," said one of the policemen.
"That's something we'd all like to know as well."

I remember to this day exactly
what Terry said, the very words:
"Jimmy riddle. I just went for a
jimmy riddle." For a moment
he even had me believing him.
What an actor! Brilliant.

We were on the bus home, right at the front on the top deck where you can guide the bus round corners all by yourself – all you have to do is steer hard on the white bar in front of you. Aunty Betty was sitting a

couple of rows behind us. Terry made quite sure she wasn't looking. Then, very surreptitiously, he took something out from under his coat and showed me. The programme.

Signed right across it were these words, which Terry read out to me:

To Terry and Andrew,
With love from your polar bear father,
Peter. Keep happy.

Night after night I asked Terry about him, and night after night under the blankets he'd tell me the story again, about how he'd gone into the dressing room and found our father sitting there in his polar bear costume with his head off (if you know what I mean), all hot and sweaty. Terry said he had a very round, very smiley face, and that he laughed just like a bear would laugh, a sort of deep bellow of a laugh – when he'd got over the surprise that is. Terry described him as looking like a "giant pixie in a bearskin".

For ever afterwards I always held it against Terry that he never took me with him that day down to the dressing room to meet my polar bear father. I was so envious. Terry had a memory of him now, a real memory. And I didn't. All I had were a few words and a signature on a theatre programme from someone I'd never even met, someone who to me was part polar bear, part actor, part pixie – not at all easy to picture in my head as I grew up.

Picture another Christmas Eve fourteen years later. Upstairs, still at the bottom of my cupboard, my polar bear father in the magazine in the Start-Rite shoebox; and with him all our accumulated childhood treasures: the signed programme, a battered champion conker (a sixty-fiver!), six silver ball bearings, four greenish silver threepenny bits (Christmas pudding treasure trove), a Red Devil throat pastille tin with three of my milk teeth cushioned in yellow cotton wool, and my collection of twenty-seven cowrie shells gleaned over many summers from the beach on Samson in the Scilly Isles.

Downstairs, the whole family were gathered in the sitting room: my mother, Douglas, Terry and my two sisters (half-sisters really, but of course no one ever called them that), Aunty Betty, now married, with twin daughters, my cousins – who were truly awful, I promise you. We were decorating the tree, or rather the twins were fighting over every single dingly-dangly glitter ball, every strand of tinsel.

I was trying to fix up the Christmas tree lights, which, of course, wouldn't work – again – whilst Aunty Betty was doing her best to avert a war by bribing the dreadful cousins away from the tree with a Mars bar each. It took a while, but in the end she got both of them up onto her lap, and soon they were stuffing themselves contentedly with Mars bars. Blessed peace.

This was the very first Christmas we had had the television. Given half a chance we'd have had it on all the time. But, wisely enough I suppose, Douglas had rationed us to just one programme a day over Christmas. He didn't want the Christmas celebrations interfered with by "that thing in the corner", as he called it. By common consent, we had chosen the Christmas Eve film on the BBC at five o'clock.

Five o'clock was a very long time coming that day, and when at last Douglas got up and turned on the television, it seemed to take for ever to warm up. Then, there it was on the screen: *Great Expectations* by Charles Dickens. The half-mended lights were at once discarded, the decorating abandoned, as we all settled down to watch in rapt anticipation. Maybe you know the moment: Young Pip is making his way through the graveyard at dusk, mist swirling around him, an owl screeching, gravestones rearing out of the gloom, branches like ghoulish fingers whipping at him as he passes, reaching out to snatch him. He moves through the graveyard timorously, tentatively, like a frightened fawn. Every snap of a twig, every

barking fox, every *aarking* heron, sends shivers into our very souls.

Suddenly, a face! A hideous face, a monstrous face, looms up from behind a gravestone. Magwitch, the escaped convict, ancient, craggy and crooked, with long white hair and a straggly beard. A wild man with wild eyes, the eyes of a wolf.

The cousins screamed in unison, long and loud, which broke the tension for all of us and made us laugh. All except my mother.

"Oh my God," she breathed, grasping my arm. "That's your father! It is. It's him. It's Peter."

All the years of pretence, the whole long conspiracy of silence, were undone in that one moment. The drama on the television paled into sudden insignificance.

The hush in the room was palpable.

Douglas coughed. "I think I'll fetch some more logs," he said. And my two half-sisters went out with him, in solidarity I think. So did Aunty Betty and the twins; and that left my mother, Terry and me alone together.

I could not take my eyes off the screen. After a while I said to Terry, "He doesn't look much like a pixie to me."

"Doesn't look much like a polar bear, either," Terry replied. At Magwitch's every appearance I tried to see through his make-up (I just hoped it *was* make-up!) to discover how my father really looked. It was impossible. My polar bear father, my pixie father, had become my convict father.

Until the credits came up at the end my mother never said a word. Then all she said was, "Well, the potatoes won't peel themselves, and I've got the Brussels sprouts to do as well." Christmas was a very subdued affair that year, I can tell you.

They say you can't put a genie back in the bottle. Not true. No one in the family ever spoke of the incident afterwards – except Terry and me, of course. Everyone behaved as if it had never happened. Enough was enough. Terry and I decided it was time to broach the whole forbidden subject with our mother, in private. We waited until the furore of Christmas was over, and caught her alone in the kitchen one evening. We asked her point-blank to tell us about him, our "first" father, our "missing" father.

"I don't want to talk about him," she said. She wouldn't even look at us. "All I know is that he lives somewhere in Canada now. It was another life. I was another person then. It's not important." We tried to press her, but that was all she would tell us.

Soon after this I became very busy with my own life, and for some years I thought very little about my convict father, my polar bear father. By the time I was thirty I was married with two sons, and was a teacher trying to become a writer, something I had never dreamt I could be.

Terry had become an actor, something he had always been quite sure he would be. He rang me very late one night in a high state of excitement. "You'll never guess," he said. "He's here! Peter! Our dad. He's here, in England. He's playing in *Henry IV, Part II* in Chichester. I've just read a rave review. He's Falstaff. Why don't we go down there and give him the surprise of his life?"

So we did. The next weekend we went down to Chichester together. I took my family with me. I wanted them to be there for this. He was a wonderful Falstaff, big and boomy, rumbustious and raunchy, yet full of pathos. My two boys (ten and eight) kept

whispering at me every time he came on. "Is that him? Is that him?" Afterwards we went round to see him in his dressing room. Terry said I should go in first, and on my own. "I had my turn a long time ago, if you remember," he said. "Best if he sees just one of us to start with, I reckon."

My heart was in my mouth. I had to take a very deep breath before I knocked on that door. "Enter." He sounded still jovial, still Falstaffian. I went in.

He was sitting at his dressing table in his vest and braces, boots and britches, and humming to himself as he rubbed off his make-up. We looked at each other in the mirror. He stopped humming, and swivelled round to face me. For some moments I just stood there looking at him. Then I said, "Were you a polar bear once, a long time ago in London?"

"Yes."

"And were you once the convict in *Great Expectations* on the television?"

"Yes."

"Then I think I'm your son," I told him.

There was a lot of hugging in his dressing room that night, not enough to make up for all those missing years, maybe. But it was a start.

My mother's dead now, bless her heart, but I still have two fathers. I get on well enough with Douglas; I always have done in a detached sort of way. He's done his best by me, I know that; but in all the years I've known him he's never once mentioned my other father. It doesn't matter now. It's history best left crusted over, I think.

We see my polar bear father – I still think of him
as that – every year or so, whenever he's over from
Canada. He's well past eighty now, still acting for six

months of every year — a real trouper. My children
and my grandchildren always call him Grandpa Bear
because of his great bushy beard (the same one he
grew for Falstaff!), and because they all know the
story of their grandfather, I suppose.

Recently I wrote a story about a polar bear. I can't imagine why. He's upstairs now reading it to my smallest granddaughter. I can hear him a-snarling and a-growling just as proper polar bears do. Takes him back, I should think.

Takes me back, that's for sure.